SECRET OMEGA

K.O. NEWMAN

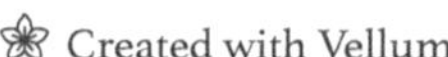 Created with Vellum

To the Sister of the Page Cafe crew. You know who you are, and I love each and every one of you.

1

CASSIE

A hundred years ago, the world ended.

Or at least that's what Veritas teaches. The entire planet went to war. A war that would scorch the earth.

And then humanity - those who survived - retreated into small clans and carried on. They rebuilt what they could and huddled down away from the destruction. They taught us to never leave our compounds, that the men outside were wild and monstrous. Nothing came in, and nothing went out.

Until the Friday just after my eighteenth birthday.

"You can't actually be considering this, Bill." I could hear momma from where I was hiding at the top of the steps. They had sent me up to my room when a gruff-looking man had come to the door.

Sue me, I was curious. I tucked myself around the corner at the top of the stairs and sat on the floor so I could hear what was being said. Men on motorcycles didn't come to our house. No one from outside of the compound came to our house. And if they did, my parents certainly wouldn't invite them in for coffee, and yet, here we were.

"What would you prefer for me to do, Matilda?" Daddy was practically yelling, which wasn't like him at all. Daddy was a soft-spoken man. He believed if people wanted to hear what you had to say, they would listen. I don't think I had ever heard him raise his voice before.

"She's our daughter," momma was saying, and I really wanted to know what they were talking about. I'm their only daughter. It's just me, no siblings.

I risked a peek down the stairs, but I could only see my parents' feet and a pair of thick black boots covered in gravel dust. He was tracking it all over momma's newly mopped floors, but she wasn't making a fuss like she did when the council came for meetings. She made them take off their shoes at the door.

"She will be well cared for," the man said. His voice was so deep I had to strain to hear it.

"Tell me how this settles my debt," Dad asked. His debt? Daddy was on the council, a high-ranking member of Veritas. We had all we needed. Why would he owe anyone?

"We pay a blood debt in blood," the man growled, his feet shifting leaving more muddy prints on momma's floors. "Her blood mixing with my son's will settle your debt."

"Bill?" I could hear the tears in momma's voice. "You can't do this. It's barbaric."

"She will be ready by Monday," daddy told a stranger who just grunted in response. "We took her off the suppressants, so she should be prepared when you get here."

Suppressants? Did he mean my medicine? Daddy said I was old enough that I didn't have to take it anymore. I was old enough that I couldn't get the sickness. But Sandy Johnson still took hers, and she was an entire month older than me.

"Monday," the stranger growled. He knocked his boots together, clods of dirt falling onto the floor before I saw him turn back to the front door. His boots might have been dirty, but his shoes looked new. Even daddy patched his boots. New was a rare luxury, everyone got hand-me-downs. "I will be here early. And I'm not waiting around, have her ready"

"Be gentle with her." Momma's voice squeaked. My parents backed towards the stairs instead of walking the stranger out. Momma was tucked up under daddy's arm, cuddled close as if the man scared her. She cleared her throat, but it still came out much higher than usual. "It will be her wedding day."

"She will be well taken care of." Coming from the stranger's mouth; it sounded more like a threat than a promise.

I curled up and pressed my back hard into the wall just at the top of the stairs in my parents' home. Wedding day? I had only just finished my studies at school. Hadn't even learned a trade yet. I would make a very poor wife.

2

DAX

My head was spinning as I threw a leg over my black Honda Shadow and kicked the engine to life. The motorcycle rumbled between my legs, sending vibrations through my entire body. Just being on my bike usually calmed my mind, but my thoughts wouldn't settle.

Marriage?

Dad had to have lost his damn mind. Sure, time was running out before my twenty-fifth birthday, but finding an omega and bonding differed from marrying some poor girl who I didn't even know and Bear hadn't scented. No one could smell as right as Hunter did.

I had a mate. He was six foot four, dirty blond hair, blue eyes, pouty lips, and covered in ink. Unfortunately, since he was also an alpha, I couldn't exactly claim him, and therefore our bears couldn't bond. For a bond, I had to find an omega. No objections, I would love a mate who could take my knot. It was hard to hold back with Hunter.

But I wanted an omega who would bond with Hunter, too. But there were no recorded triad bonds. Science was still out on a lot about dynamics. After a century we were still shooting in the dark about the changes that had happened after the last World War.

History said that bombs rained down and governments fell. From the ashes a new order had risen, which put me at the top of the food chain. Well, not me personally, but Motorcycle clubs, mafia, militia. Anyone who could enforce the orders they laid down. Might ruled the land. And the Kodiak Motorcycle Club, Lone Bear Chapter, owned my little slice of the world. Those who didn't live within the system hid away in compounds. There was only one such compound in Lone Bear, and they paid protection fees to the Kodiak.

The purr of Hunter's bike beside mine pulled me out of my contemplation. I nodded at him. I had until Monday to fix this crazy idea dad had come up with. Not just any omega could bond with me, Bear wouldn't stand for it. And where better to think than the seat of my bike with the growl of the engine between my thighs. Or I could avoid thinking, with my cock shoved down Hunter's throat.

I tried to ignore the scent of damp air. If I wasn't mistaken, we had just enough time to get to the cabin, if we rode fast. The switchbacks on Lone Bear Peak were wicked under pleasant conditions. Wet? They would be a nightmare on a bike. The winding mountain roads were no joke. Even for the most experienced rider, and a smart man wouldn't attempt it when it was slick with rain and mud. But I never claimed to be smart. Not to mention I needed space from the eyes of the club. The Kodiak MC was my world, it was my clan, but they were also a bunch of nosy ass bear shifters without omegas to settle them. Too many alphas and not enough omegas to go around. And with mom out of her breeding years, she could no longer be the clan omega. It was my turn to step up. They would be all up in my business while I looked for an omega to take care of, or for dad to force one on me.

Just the thought of bonding to an omega that wasn't right made my stomach turn. Sure, she would settle the betas, but if she mated me, she would push Hunter out of the clan. Dad wouldn't be an issue, he was bonded. But Hunter would be another alpha in her territory and unless he found his own omega. I shook my head to dislodge those thoughts. No one I mated would push Hunter away. I wouldn't allow it. I dared a look behind me at the headlamp of Hunter's bike keeping pace with mine. Bear growled low inside of me. He wanted Hunter and his bear right by our side. Fuck finding an omega.

I pulled my jacket tighter over my chest and ran a finger over the space where my VP patch had been. Marry the girl and get it back, dad had said, when he ripped it off two days ago. Marry the girl and claim her before the club.

But what about Bear? I would lose control of Bear if I claimed an omega that didn't smell right. If I lost Bear, I would definitely lose my spot in the clan. An out-of-control animal was a one-way ticket to hell. Claiming the omega would mean losing Hunter.

If I lost Hunter, I would absolutely lose myself.

I could be dead on the inside, mated to an omega I didn't want or dead on the outside without a clan in the wilds. Choices, choices.

I looked at Hunter where he sat astride his Rebel. His Sergeant at Arms patch was still secured to his chest, but where I go, so went his nation. If I lost my place with the MC, he would go rogue with me, and we would take our betas. Losing six members at once could cripple the clan.

I blew out off the main street and down the dirt mountain road. I didn't have to look to know that Hunter was right in step behind me. The roar of our bikes blocked everything else out as we slowed to round curves up the side of Lone Bear Peak.

I took a breath of cool air as it blasted against my face, the deep scent of pine filling me up. Bear was still manageable. At some point I would have to do something, make a claim, but I had plenty of time to find a mate and tether Bear to an omega who smelled right, an omega who would love Hunter like I do. Right?

The closer we got to the peak, the lower the temperature dropped. I could smell rain on the wind and saw the first drops of icy cold water in the air. I pushed my bike faster, wanting to make it to the cabin before the first drizzle turned into proper drops. There was a storm brewing, and when storms blew in, so did trouble.

I needed one more weekend with Hunter.

I looked over my shoulder to see the same concentration on Hunter's face as we made the last turn. Just one weekend where it was just me and Hunter, then I would face this girl dad had found me. And Bear and I would make a choice.

Dead on the inside, or dead on the outside.

3

CASSIE

I popped the parking brake on daddy's car and eased it down the driveway. My daddy was one of the few who even owned a car, and because gasoline was so precious, I had never learned to drive it. Luckily, I had seen daddy do it often enough, and I was desperate enough that I would figure it out. Looking at the myriad of pedals and levers made my heart race. But necessity is the mother of ingenuity, or something. Right?

Once I was out on the street outside the compound, I got in the car and pointed it towards the mountains. I had never left home, none of us ever did. Daddy said it was safer, but I wasn't so sure anymore. Not after the stranger came to the house.

Uncle Titus, momma's brother, used to talk about a cabin up on Lone Bear Peak that his grandfather had owned, back before the sickness. I had seen maps and pictures of the old place. But in the darkness, the world looked so much bigger than I had ever imagined. The mountains looked so imposing from out here, and the road stretched on forever.

I turned up the volume on the radio and drove to the crooning voice of some old song about thunder that was particularly fitting. I could already feel the charge in the air that promised lightning, and the faraway rumble that told me trouble was coming. Normally, I would be at home, chasing the chickens back into the coop or helping momma get the wash off the line. I would never do that again, not now that I had left. Once you left, you couldn't go back.

The Veritas Compound was terrified of the illness that lived outside the compound. We were told that it had corrupted the entire world once, that we'd only been saved from the mighty force of demons by locking ourselves away. Veritas's teachers taught us that when the bombs fell, they brought with them an illness that swept the Earth, and the destruction it brought ended the world.

When I imagined what it would look like outside the compound, I had always envisioned rusted out, and rotting cars lining the streets, garbage blowing across a road filled with potholes, and weeds growing wild. I found none of that. The streets were straight and clean, the yellow lines down the center were bright in the headlights of daddy's car, and the roads were empty of any vehicles.

I was barely a mile from the compound when the first drops of rain fell. I had to pull over to the side of the road and find the lever for the windshield wipers. Once I was at the cabin, if I could even find it, I would build a warm fire and plan my next move. I couldn't live forever in a cabin in the woods, after all.

What the hell were my parents talking about with that stranger? He definitely wasn't from Veritas. I knew everyone, and he looked too rough. Daddy was breaking the rules, letting someone into the compound from the outside. If people started getting sick, they would punish daddy. I could just see daddy in the stalks in the middle of the square as rain poured down from the heavens. Momma would lose her status, the whole family would. It would mean no more big house, and no more fresh meat for Sunday dinner, amongst other things. I almost felt sad, but then I remembered daddy was selling me to a stranger. And marriage? I had only just turned eighteen. I don't want to marry anyone.

I cranked up the speed on the wipers as I turned onto the one lane road that wound up Lone Bear Peak. Even the road signs looked new and shiny as I passed them. Clearly things on the outside differed greatly from what daddy and our teachers had told us. There had to be people out here. Not just monsters and wild men.

I gripped the steering wheel with white knuckles and leaned forward to see through the deluge. There was no turning around, there was no going back. So forward it was, even as the wiper blades streaked grime over the old windshield, and the rain thrummed on the roof like the drumming of hooves.

I slowed the ancient Toyota to a crawl as the storm poured down around me, the wipers barely keeping up as they made a mess of the windshield, and the road was getting harder and harder to see the darker it got. And even when I squinted so hard my face hurt, the lines of the road were washed to nothing in the deluge. I turned off the radio and hunched further over the steering wheel, but it was no use. I crept along the road, using the trees on either side as a guide.

Just another mile, I chanted under my breath. Slow and steady. I killed the engine over and over while trying to creep along. The lurching of the engine stalling made my heart leap into my throat each time. My hands shook as I turned the key again and pressed on the gas, releasing the clutch only to have it lurch to a stop again moments later. As I rounded a sharp turn, it nearly brought me to tears. Just one more mile. I wiped my cheeks with the back of my hand and took a deep breath. I could do this, I had to.

Water flooded over the windshield. I could feel the tires struggling to grip the old mountain road as a river of rain spilled down the cliffs. My hands ached as I went around another hairpin turn as slowly as I could, riding the clutch so hard I could smell it filling the cabin of the car. The tires slid in the mud running down the mountainside and across the road, and I clutched the wheel with everything I had, my teeth grinding together as I forced the car another inch up the mountain.

I held my breath until I felt the wheels catch the road again and the car straighten out. I let out a sigh of relief. Slow and steady. I wasn't in any rush to get to the cabin, except the needle on the gas gauge was a little worrisome. Daddy rarely filled the tank, and now it was deep in the red. Just one more mile.

The tires lost traction with a fresh wave of watery mud that slipped across the road, and the car spun to the right, so fast I nearly hit my head on the window.

I hit the brakes and wrenched the wheel. The engine died, and my heart stopped. The car kept going, directly towards the trees that lined the side of the road. My fingers clawed at the wheel, turning it this way and that, but nothing happened.

My breath caught in my throat as the bumper hit the ancient guardrail. I could almost hear the metal straining against the force of the car. But then it ricocheted off the rail, spinning back towards the trees. I pressed my feet into the clutch and brake, jamming the levers into the floor as I turned the key over and over. The engine made a sickening screech each time I turned the key, but it wouldn't start. I could feel my heart beating up in my throat as the trees got closer.

Then there was a thump as the back wheels slid off the edge of the road. Pain blossomed in my head where it struck against the driver's side window, and then the world went dark when something exploded out of the steering wheel.

4

DAX

The cabin in the woods wasn't much. Just a single room with a wood-burning stove for heat and cooking, a couch, a small dining set, and a bed. But it was the perfect place to hide out from dad and figure out how I would get out of marrying some poor human girl I had never met. How would I keep from losing Hunter? Bear paced inside of me, begging to be let out. I could solve anything while hunting, and Bear wanted blood.

Hunter rested lazily on the bed, his shirt and cut with the Kodiak MC patch and rockers on obvious display draped over the chair, and his boots on the floor next to the door. He idly threw a tennis ball up into the air and caught it. He looked like the picture of relaxation, and only the low growl I could hear coming from his chest, let me know Beast was as riled up as Bear was. I looked over at him as I dropped onto the bed next to him. His bare chest with dark lines of ink curling over his thick muscles glowed in the kerosene lamp's light. One of his hands was folded under his head, a faraway look in his blue eyes. The moment my skin touched his, Bear settled.

"Just mate Jasmine." Hunter made a face, not looking at me. I know how much he didn't like Jasmine, and as far as I could tell, the feeling was mutual. "I mean, it's not ideal, but then you at least keep your place as VP." He shrugged like it was that easy. Jasmine didn't like him, which made her a no-go. Plus, I didn't like Jasmine. She smelled like cheap perfume and stale sex. I wouldn't be able to make a claim stick, not that I wanted to put my mouth anywhere near her skin. Just the thought made Bear cringe.

"I'm not mating Jasmine." She was a Kitten. Not an actual cat, that would be cute. Cat shifters were adorable, if vicious. No, Jasmine was a biker groupie and beta who had unfortunately latched on to me, much to the annoyance of everyone involved. She had great tits and could definitely fill out a pair of jeans. For a quick fuck she was fine for most of the guys, but the girl had nothing going on between her ears. Not to mention, her voice made Bear cringe. "She smells wrong, and she can't take my knot. If I want to keep you, I have to find a nice omega who doesn't mind that you and I come as a package deal. We have enough betas between us."

"It will not happen, man." Hunter rolled his head towards me with a sad look on his face. "No omega will agree to taking on two alphas. And Bear will not like my scent all over your claim, anyhow."

No omega would want to deal with two rutting alphas every time she went into heat. That's why we have betas to help. Two alphas? Two knots? That would be too much for any girl, even an omega who was built to take us. But I wanted that. I wanted Hunter to love my omega the way I knew I would. And if they really meant her to be mine, she would love Hunter because I did. Right? And Hunter was wrong, Bear would love his scent on our omega. I loved Hunter's scent all over me, so what would be the difference? Hunter smelled like warm pine needles and freshly turned earth, just like the air around the cabin. It was home to me. But would it still smell like home when it was rubbed all over an omega?

Not if it was some omega dad had tracked down. I wouldn't want to share Hunter with her. If she smelled wrong, I wouldn't want her to touch him.

"Yeah." I sighed and leaned back on the bed, my hands laced over my head as I looked up at the wooden ceiling. "So, we have until Monday, and I'm saddled with an omega I have to try to bond, and then present to our clan?"

"We should absolutely take advantage of our time." Hunter rolled towards me and pulled at the buckle of my belt.

"That sounds like a fantastic idea," I growled and pulled him into a rough kiss, my fingers fisting into his hair as he bit at my lips. Bear was in heaven. Hunter was ours.

5

CASSIE

The throbbing in my skull woke me up. I pushed the moldy material that had spilled out of the steering wheel and winced as I turned the key to pull the car back onto the road, but the engine just made a sick noise and died. I leaned my head on the wheel and took a long slow breath, trying to calm my heart after the system dump of adrenaline coursing through my veins.

God, was I lucky. I felt around my hairline, looking for injuries, but other than the knot on my head from where I had hit the window, I was fine.

I pulled a pair of mittens out of the glove box and stuffed my hands in them. I climbed out of the car carefully and looked at the damage. The back tires were completely off the road and were hanging in midair. Great, I was stuck.

I slid back behind the wheel of the car and leaned my head on the headrest, counting to ten slowly. I was just going to walk the rest of the way.

I pulled off my gloves and reached gingerly into the back seat for my bag. Rain was falling in fat drops through the open door. Water had already soaked through my clothes. With a sigh, I pulled my bag into my lap and zipped my coat up tight, like it would help. I stuffed my hands back into my sodden mittens and got out of the car.

The rain made it nearly impossible to find my way. Ice cold drops stung my eyes. The wind drove my drenched hair against my face, and I fought the urge to cry again. It wouldn't do any good.

I huddled into my coat, tucking my chin into my chest and breathing down into the fabric as water ran down into the jacket and soaked my sweater underneath. The longer I walked, the colder it got. My fingers and toes were numb, and it got harder to lift my soaking legs out of the muddy earth. They were so cold they burned.

Finally, up ahead, I saw a light.

Or I thought it was a light? I tried to blink water out of my eyes and get a better look, but it was no use.

I felt like I had a million humming birds in my chest, my breath squeezing out of my chest as I watched that light bobbing in the darkness in front of me. I pressed my fingers into my jaw, rubbing where I had been gritting my teeth so hard my face ached, in an effort just to keep my teeth from clacking together.

The light was still so far in the distance, and it was so cold. I tried to run towards the light, but my shoes slipped in the deepening mud, and I fell face first into the mud as my legs buckled under me. As I tried to get my feet under me, I slipped and slid. I shook the worst of the mud off of my sleeves, using my hands to slop the mud to the ground, letting the rain take care of the rest.

It felt like forever before I made it to a small porch of a log cabin. There was smoke coming up from the chimney, so someone had to be home.

I knocked and sank against the doorframe. Drops of muddy water ran down my body, my white jacket an ugly brown that seeped rain to my sweater underneath. I tried to keep my eyes open for just another minute. It would have been so easy to just close them right there, to just let sleep take me.

HUNTER

"Fuck," Dax grumbled as I pulled away, his hands trying to grab me as I slipped from the bed. There's no place I would rather be, but if someone was knocking on the door... "It's just the tree hitting the fucking porch again. Come back to bed." He rolled onto his back and fisted his dick with one hand while beckoning me with the other. Dax slowly slid his hand up to the tip and flicked his wrist before pushing his cock back into the ring he'd made with his fingers, his eyes never leaving mine. Fuck, he could be such an asshole.

I groaned. But I absolutely had heard something, and it was too heavy to be the tree branch. I had cut those back the last time we were here for that exact reason. "Just let me check, man." I wrapped a throw blanket around my hips and stalked over to the door, while Dax made exaggerated moaning sounds from the bed. I loved him, but seriously. As I unlocked the door, I flipped him off.

The door blasted open with the force of the wind and standing in the deluge on the porch was a girl. She was wet through and shaking with the cold. But I forgot all of that when her scent wafted in behind her. Spun cinnamon sugar. If my dick hadn't already been hard, it would have been with one whiff of her amazing scent.

The girl half frozen on our porch was an omega, and by the way her scent kept getting sweeter, she was close to her heat. Man, we were screwed.

Beast stirred inside me and blinked. I could feel him rumble as he sniffed the air, the sound vibrating through my chest. He wanted this girl. I could feel his need to claim her riding up my throat.

As the door smacked against the wall, she practically fell into my arms, covering us both in a layer of mud and rain, sending a shiver up my spine. Her little button nose and delicate cheeks were badly windburned, and her full lips looked like they were turning blue. I kicked the door closed, pulling her tighter to my chest. A zing of recognition rode my skin as I pulled her further into the cabin.

"Not the wind, asshole," I shouted over my shoulder and helped the omega over to the fire. "Put your dick away dude, and bank up this fire."

"I'm sorry to interrupt." The girl chattered, lifting her face up to look at me. Something hit me in the chest like a bowling ball. God, she was pretty, with her big blue eyes, and porcelain skin. And she smelled so good, I just wanted to rub myself all over her, cover her with my scent. Beast wanted to mark her up and keep her. He roared inside me to bite her before anyone else could smell her, whispering promises of sharing her heat with Bear and Dax. Of her swelling, round with our child.

Her wide blue eyes caught mine, and they burned through me. Beast growled, which I quickly covered with a cough. She didn't seem to notice. Her eyes were glassy, either with her preheat riding her skin, or the hypothermia that she was in danger of being consumed by, neither of which were good.

"I got turned around," she said, her voice quiet. She was trying to stand back up on her own feet, but was doing more flailing helplessly than anything, her knees not bothering to support her weight. I tightened my hold around her waist, pressing her full round breasts against my chest harder, and hooked one of her flapping arms around my shoulders. Trying mostly in vain to keep the blanket around me. It didn't really matter, we would need to get her out of her wet clothes and against warm skin, anyway. And fast. A shower wouldn't go amiss. Her clothes were filthy.

"What on earth were you doing out there on foot?" I pulled her toward the wood stove and opened the front, pushing in another log and glaring at Dax, who was still rolling out of bed. "Take off those clothes." I hitched my blanket around my hips and reached for the zipper of her coat.

"I can do it myself." Her teeth clacked together, and her fingers shook so badly that she couldn't even grip the slider. Her long dark hair tumbled in a mass over her shoulder and seemed to tangle around her arms as she tried to grab the zipper. She gave off a very human growl and shook her hand out. It was so fucking cute. "Gosh darn it." She was absolutely adorable looking all frustrated, her little nose all wrinkled up. I resisted the urge to press my cheek to hers, and leave my scent on her, try to calm the racing of her heart with my alpha scent.

Beast begged me to help her, to take care of her, to rub my face against hers and cover her scent with mine, get drunk off the pheromones she was soaking the air with. To bite her and shove my face in her pussy so I could smell her constantly, and taste that cinnamon sugar on my lips. I shook my head, trying to dislodge those thoughts.

She shook her hand out again, her thin, delicate fingers were so white they were almost blue, trying to grasp the pull of her zipper. In the end she looked at me in defeat, her enormous eyes brimmed with tears. I couldn't help but chuckle, I risked scaring her, and placed a quick kiss on her cheek, and Beast crooned when she let me pull the zip down, wafting me in more of her cinnamon sugar scent along with the faint taste of her pheromones on my lips.

Under the heavy coat, her clothes were soaked through. I could see her pink bra clearly through her translucent white shirt, even with a layer of mud. She shook with cold, and I chastised myself for thinking about getting my mouth on her skin. And not hurrying to get her warm. My mate needed me to take care of her first.

"Wood outside is soaked, Hunter." Dax stomped up behind the girl, and she startled, pressing her full tits against my chest. Probably because he hadn't bothered to put fucking pants on. He stood there looking at her, his dick swinging at half mast between his thighs. And yeah, she was definitely looking, cause the parts of her that weren't red before, definitely were when she took in Dax's massive cock. She took a deep breath of the scent coming from Dax, and her eyes went hazier.

Beast was even more excited about that. Her scent was thick in the air. She was looking at what was ours. She would be an excellent mate. I shook my head again, and eased her jacket off her shoulders, dropping it on the floor with a wet smack.

7

CASSIE

"I umm..." I put my hands over my eyes and hummed. Oh my god, what did I just stumble into? Cause those were the two most perfect specimens of a man I had ever seen, and they both seemed to feel like clothing was optional.

The blond one in the blanket had the most enchanting blue eyes and tattoos that curled around his muscles. I had never seen a man with muscles like his. His forearms were as thick as my thighs, and he was down on his knees in front of me, tugging off my boots, while keeping me upright with a massive hand on my waist. I could have sworn that his fingers were sending little electric pulses through my body each time we touched. And all I wanted to do was reach out and trace the lines of ink on his skin. I wanted to sink my hands in his thick hair and rub his face against mine until he was all I could smell. I wanted to feel the blond scruff on his face rasping against my skin.

The dark-haired naked man was just as impressive. He was just a little taller than the blond and had far more

25

tattoos. They climbed down his chest, over his hands, and to his hairline. He was standing over, hands on his hips, full eight pack abs glowing in the lantern light, and his dick was practically pointing at me. Dear me. That was quite a cock. Long, thick, and not even fully erect.

I felt hot and cold all over, and something wet gushed between my thighs and I pressed them hard together. The scent of pine and cloves was thick in the cabin, and it was making my head swim. But that could also have just been the fact that I was shivering so hard it was difficult to stay standing. My face felt feverish, burning even. My thighs were sticky with arousal. That had absolutely never happened before.

"I really am so sorry for interrupting," I almost whispered, my voice stuck in my throat as the scent of Christmas trees grew thicker the closer the two men got to me. I tried not to stare at either of the men. Instead of tracing the lines of in on their arms while the blond worked my sodden socks off my feet. There were so many patterns, whirls and flowers, and a fiery skull that flowed off his shoulder and down onto the blond's chest. His skin felt so good against my ice cold instep. I had never thought having my feet touched would be sexy, but his touch went straight to my center, making me tingle. "It's just terrible out there, and I was lost, and your light was on."

"Nothing to apologize for, sweetheart. Dax's just being an asshole." Blondie glared at Dax. "Put your dick away, dude, you're scaring her."

Not scared. A little intimidated, cause it was not even completely hard, and it looked like a fucking tree trunk. Just thinking about it made me ache in my middle, but definitely not scared. I placed my hand on blondie's shoulder as I wobbled a bit, and a zing of electricity went up my arm. I shook out the pins and needles. Shouldn't have any static with me being so wet. Blondie made an indistinct sound in the back of his throat, his hand tightening on my waist. I almost missed the satisfied look on his face. Weird. I usually hated getting shocked, but all I wanted to do was touch him again and feel that release of electricity.

"I was very much using it before she knocked on the door," Dax mumbled quietly enough that I was mostly sure that he wasn't expecting me to hear, but the hazy look in his eyes made the words sting less. I felt terrible for interrupting their naked time. Though they could have gone right back to it, I would not have minded watching. Oh god, I had not just thought that. "Fuck. Get her warm, she's shaking."

"Asshole's just grumpy, cause ya smell so good, and Bear's probably all kinds of confused," blondie whispered loudly to me. I just nodded at him like I had any clue what he was talking about. Then, I couldn't seem to stop once I started. I just shivered and nodded like a crazy person, while tracing the lines of ink on his skin with my eyes. In flourished cursive, right over his heart, in amongst the rays of a sun was the name 'Dax'. His entire right arm inked in intricate little designs and words, too, and I wanted to touch every inch.

It was much warmer in the cabin than it had been outside, but I was soaked through, right down to my panties. And blondie was slowly tugging my clothes off and dumping them into a pile by the door.

"Yeah, he wants his dick sucked, and I ruined it." My voice shook with the force of my chattering. *You could offer to help,* my brain supplied unhelpfully. I slapped my band over my mouth, shocked at what had just come out of it. *Oh my god, shut up.* "I am so sorry."

"He'll get over it." Blondie grinned up at me, then looked down expectantly at the fly of my jeans. Yeah, they should probably come off too, along with my soaked shirt, which was one hundred percent see through, and showing off my bright pink bra to the world. *Did my breasts look bigger? Must be the shaking.*

"Really, cause most guys I know would milk that shit." I mumbled, while I shrugged out of my unbuttoned sweater, leaving me in just my shirt.

"Gotta get out of those jeans, too, princess." Blondie's hand hovered over the zip on my jeans and looked at me again with a question in his eyes. Brushing away his hand. I tried and fumbled with this zipper. *I could really take off my own pants, I did it basically every day.* My hand shook so badly that it took a few tries before I could even grip the slider. I got the zip halfway down, and it stuck. *Cause of course it did.*

"Really?" I growled in frustration and yanked at the fabric, trying to rip the material from the tiny metal teeth. "My day is seriously not going my way." I sat down on the floor in defeat, feeling the sting of tears pricking at the corners of my eyes. I sniffed.

I would not start crying again. I was away from Veritas, and could never go home. But no one would sell me away to be married to some gross stranger. So, my day was going better than it had started out, right?

"Can I help now?" he asked, his voice soft. He took my hands between his and brought them to his lips, kissing my fingers gently.

Dax was still standing there, dick out, watching us with a weird look in his eyes, like he didn't know if he should help or eat us both. I shivered under his scrutiny, with this urge to turn over and push my hind side up to him. The thought made my middle tingle, and I saw his eyes darken. Eyes that looked brown when I first looked at him, but were now a wintery gray and shining eerily in the light. It had to be the kerosene lamps.

Hallucinations were normal with hypothermia, right? I blinked a few times, but the gray just seemed to gleam in the light like a cat's.

"I am so sorry, my name is Cassie." I turned my hand in blondie's and gripped it properly, palm to palm. His hands were so much bigger than mine, that I could barely see my fingers wrapping around the sides of his palm. He grinned at me and shook my hand. Brief jolts danced along my fingers and straight down to my core. I could feel more sticky wetness seep from between my legs, and I fought the urge to rub my thighs together.

"Hunter." Hunter pointed over his shoulder to where Dax was watching us, not bothering to cover himself. His dick wasn't half mast anymore. And now I was intimidated, because he didn't look angry or upset that I was there anymore, he looked hungry. And I should not be looking at the man's penis, but I couldn't help it. I pulled my hand out of Hunter's and covered my eyes, feeling my cheeks heat. "That asshole, again, is Dax."

"Boyfriend?" I asked, talking to Hunter but peeking through my fingers, trying not to look at Dax who was basically waving his peen in my face, a gleam in his eyes that told me he wanted me to look. This was not a big cabin, and I had two naked men, one of which was working on the stuck zipper of my jeans. I had died in the storm. That was the only explanation. I heard the fabric of my pants rip and groaned.

"Kind of?" Hunter hedged. "It's kind of not talked about."

"Huh." I peeked between my fingers again and was only partially relieved that Dax had finally turned around, giving me a view of his tight ass instead of his swinging dick. Improvement? "Just between you and me, if I had a man that fine, I would crow it from the rooftops." Men from Veritas did not look like these two. They both looked like those statues in old school art books. The men at Veritas didn't have six-pack abs, or long thick hair, and none of them had tattoos. No, the men at home were all too thin, and none of them had the bulging muscles. I cocked my head to one side and looked Hunter up and down. Yep, boiling, and the thought of those two together. My thighs were so wet that I knew the moment Hunter pulled my jeans down, he could tell. What on god's green earth was wrong with me? "He should shout from the rooftops, too. Just saying."

"Cassie, I think this is the start of a beautiful friendship." Hunter helped me out of the jeans he had torn open, and a shiver ran through my body as fingers grazed the skin of my thighs as he worked the sodden material down my legs. His touch felt like pure electricity. My face heated as his hands rubbed down my legs, like he couldn't keep from touching me. I fought to keep from letting my knees fall open, and just inviting him in. Good girls did not spread their legs for boys. That's what momma and daddy had always told me. Dutiful daughters waited for marriage, so that god would approve, and it wouldn't be a sin. But, god, they made me want to sin. I wanted to open my legs and pull Hunter into me. I wanted my sticky wetness all over him, so he smelled like me.

Something was very wrong with me, because I had wanted nothing like that before. I had never ached like if someone didn't touch me I would die. I never wanted a man in my life, and there I was, trying to keep from begging two strangers to touch me, so my body would stop aching for it.

Hunter's eyes flashed in the lamplight as they met mine. Not blue, like I thought, but gray, a warm gray with flecks of gold, they shone in the light. His eyes were on the juncture of my thighs, and I just knew he could hear my thoughts, knew I wanted him to put his fingers on me, and rub until I exploded.

"Might wanna wrap that blanket around her too, Hunter," Dax growled from where he was trying to pull all the blankets off the bed at once. "Wouldn't wanna let our little guest die of hypothermia."

"You wanna bring those blankets and cuddle with us?" Hunter canted his head at his boyfriend, pulling the blanket around my shoulders. His fingers grazed my skin, and I rubbed into his touch. A rumbling growl came from his throat, so I did it again, rubbing my skin against his, a brief smile pulling at my lips when he grazed the top of my head with his chin.

"This is our last weekend," Dax pouted. Oh, no. I felt like absolute grit. I was nuzzling all over Hunter, and here he was with Dax. I almost offered to go back into the rain, just so they could be alone, but Hunter tucked me under his arm, and he was so warm and smelled so good. Pine needles and male flooded my senses. I had never wanted to bathe in someone's scent before. All I wanted to do was dig in and wrap myself around his heated skin. I was like one of the barn cats when they went into heat. Daddy told me that those urges were wrong, but it felt so good to touch Hunter. I bet Dax would feel good, too. If only he would stop frowning at me. "I just... Fuck, we gotta get her warm."

"Yeah, I get it." Hunter looked down at me, while I looked back and forth between the guys in bewilderment. "Dax is engaged."

"To a girl?" I ask. Hunter carefully pulled me down to the floor, all wrapped up in his blanket, even though I was still in my wet shirt and panties. He encased us together under the blanket. I had never felt so safe and cared for. He tucked me up tight against his chest, and I couldn't help but rub my face against him.

Something was clearly wrong with my brain, I barely know these guys. They could be axe murderers for all I knew. Holed up in this mountain cabin waiting for unsuspecting girls to stumble on them. Daddy had said that the men outside of Veritas were monsters. And I was just playing right into their hands, practically placing myself on a plate and serving up whatever they wanted.

"Yeah. It's not a problem. Dax likes girls just fine." He shrugged. "I do too," he whispered against the side of my neck. My dear goodness. My insides were seriously melting. "It's just with each other..." Hunter left the sentence hanging, watching me carefully to see what I did, I guess. Yep, I one thousand percent wanted to watch them together. For reasons. "Sometimes with a girl, too." He winked.

Another gush of stickiness flowed out of me, and my head went swimmy for a moment. It was the cold; it was making me sick. Had to be. My entire body was reacting to every touch, every look. It was too hot, and yet perfect under the blanket with Hunter. I wanted Dax under the blanket too. I needed more skin touching me.

"Ah." I just smiled at him, like an idiot. What they did in their personal time was none of my business. I would just keep to myself that I wanted to watch them bang. God brain, shut up, not helpful. I groaned and went to bury my head and hide, but hiding my face against Hunter's perfect chest did not help my pervy brain, cause now I wanted to sink my teeth into his perfect pecs, and never let go. Goodness, he smelled good. Like wood smoke and pine and sexy man. "I'm kind of engaged too."

"To a girl?" Hunter teased, his cheek rubbing against the top of my head, a growl coming from his lips. I tried to swallow a whine that tore up my throat, but I couldn't. Hunter pulled me closer, his gigantic hand spanning the top of my thigh as he squeezed it gently.

"Ha!" I needed to get away from all his skin or I would do something really embarrassing. "No, at least I don't think so." I snuggled closer and rubbed the side of my face against his chest, then froze. Something embarrassing like that. But a rumble came from Hunter's chest again, that said he hadn't minded.

"You don't know?" Dax joined us from the bedroom area, pulling the thick cover with him like a cloak. "Some kind of arranged marriage?"

"Something like that." I tucked myself further under Hunter's arm, trying to chase every bit of warmth I could. I couldn't get close enough to him. He was a complete stranger, but my body wanted to slide all over him. Hunter just wrapped me tighter in his arms and grabbed Dax's hand. "Apparently I will meet him next week, I didn't stick around to hear all the details."

Hunter looked at Dax and raised a brow. They had a silent conversation that I don't understand, then Hunter turned to me. "Well, then you can join us in our 'avoiding the nuptials' weekend."

"I would be happy to, and only partially because I don't really have a choice." I looked over at Dax, then back at Hunter. Both had wide, surprised grins on their faces. "Is it a clothing optional weekend?" I teased, looking between us in our stages of undress. Hunter's jaw had to have hit the floor, he looked so shocked.

I was about to retract my statement when Dax interrupted my backpedaling. "Fuck, Cassie." Dax grinned at me, tucking me between him and Hunter, and then pulled Hunter in for a long kiss over my head, his hand squeezing the thigh that Hunter didn't have in his grip, encasing me between them. "I don't have any objections to a naked party, and only partially because you really need to get out of those wet clothes so you don't get sick." He gave me a sexy boy wink, and I wanted to melt. I didn't take my eyes off of him as I pulled my shirt over my head and let it drop with a wet plop onto the floor outside of our little cocoon.

8

DAX

Cassie had the most perfectly round tits that bounced when she giggled, which Hunter had been making her do for the last half hour. She was the most beautiful and best smelling omega I could ever have imagined. She had this cute little nose that turned up right at the tip, and eyes that were so blue. Her hair had dried in the cabin's warmth, and was golden brown, tumbling in loose curls across Hunter's chest. The scent of cinnamon sugar and pine and cloves filled the cabin around me and Bear wanted to roll around in it.

I'd been trying to play it cool, because we were trying to get her warmed up - we did not want her to get hypothermia this far from the clubhouse and Doc - not riled up, but I just couldn't stop touching her. Her skin was so soft, with lush hips that fit in the palm of my hand like they were meant to be there, and the little electric shocks zipped along my skin every time my fingers played along the tops of her bare, round thighs. I watched how her perfect rosebud nipples puckered with just a glance, and the scent of her slick was thick in the air. I licked my lips, trying to chase her pheromones on my tongue.

I think I might have fallen in love.

Hunter was sitting with her still tucked under his arm, his eyes glued to her chest like he'd never seen a pair of tits before. He held her close to his chest, and rubbed his chin over the crown of her head, rubbing his scent into her hair. The girl attached to them was what pulled my attention. She had a beautiful laugh, full and rich, not a single fake note.

Cassie's smell was just getting stronger the longer she was touching Hunter and me. Her heat was fast approaching, and she didn't seem to notice. She was just tucked up between us, her fingers hesitant to skim over our skin, but ever once in a while, her hand would reach out and pet me. She kept her touch so neutral, just like brushes along my arm, or rub her cheek against Hunter's, leaving a trail of her scent on his skin. I could hear Beast purring.

She looked natural, cuddled up under a blanket between the two of us. It felt right to have her touching us and letting us touch her. Bear was so close to the surface I could feel him rubbing up against my insides, trying to rub his scent on her skin. With each passing second — the thicker her pheromones grew in the tiny cabin — I wanted her more. I needed her like I needed Hunter. The way I had never needed someone else before.

She was my omega. My mate.

She smelled fucking fantastic with Hunter all over her. She would only smell better when we marked her. When our scent mixed with hers, and she wore our scars on her throat. I was way ahead of myself, but I didn't care. My teeth ached to pierce her skin, to seal my scent inside of her. I wanted my hands on her full hips, my cock deep inside her, knot blown, tying us together. A growl rumbled up my throat as I looked down at her sweet face.

"So, you're getting sold as a breeder?" I prompted, shoving the growl back down my throat. Bear did not like thinking about someone else touching her, someone doing something as crass as buying an omega to breed. I wasn't a fan of the skin trade. They traded betas and Gammas like cattle, especially Gammas, who were treated like toys. But an Omega? Omegas were so rare, and so precious. The thought of someone trading for one? I was sick enough that my father was trying to do the same thing.

It had to be a coincidence; I reminded myself. I couldn't be the only person in the world who was being set up with an omega I don't know. Plus, dad had gone to one of those human communes to find me a bride. Those compounds were just farms in the country where humans held themselves up and pretended like gender dynamics weren't a thing. Pretended that the last war hadn't changed everything. Pretended that science hadn't fucked with our genes just because they could.

"A breeder?" She pulled slightly away from Hunter, pushing her hand against his chest as he tried to pull her back.

Fuck. "Yeah, you know, a mail-order bride, darling?" I watched her for any recognition. It was more common for a beta or gamma's parents to sell them off to clans - parents prayed for a child who was anything but a gamma - but it happened to omegas, too. There was worry but no spark of recognition in her face. Shit. Did she not know what she was? I would bet Bear himself that she didn't even know she was in heat.

"Oh, yeah. Apparently." Her giggles stopped, and her scent went acrid for a moment and made Bear want to retch with the scent of her distress. We needed to fix it. She picked at her fingers, her blue eyes full of emotion, swirling uncomfortably as she struggled to meet my eyes. "I heard my parents talking to someone about my wedding day. Something about suppressants? I mean I've been on medication my entire life, everyone takes it. But nothing they said made any sense. I heard arranged marriage and kind of crawled out of my bedroom window."

"Good call." Hunter hugged her tighter to his chest, tucking the blanket around us and closing our scents into the fabric. Her eyes dipped to his lap, then quickly away, a light blush dusting her porcelain cheeks. Her scent was sweet again, and Bear settled back to rubbing inside of me, wanting to mark her, make her ours. "Dax has known for over a year he's marrying someone. But Daddy dearest has been tight-lipped on who it is."

"Why?" she asked. And it was a fair question, but I didn't even know how to answer it.

Most alphas wouldn't hear of being given an omega they didn't choose. Betas did it because they were not driven by scent. They could mate whoever they wanted. An alpha not choosing a mate? It was killing Bear to think they would pair me with an omega that might not smell right. If she didn't smell right, I couldn't bond her, and if I couldn't bond her, we would never have cubs. She would just be a trophy piece that could would be shown off. Having an omega in a clan was a status symbol. But I wanted more. Bear craved cubs, it was alpha instinct. And Bear wanted Cassie to have our cubs. Bear wanted Cassie to have Hunter's cubs. Bond her to us unequivocally and stay round with our children.

"I mean it's not my business, but I'm curious." I continued. She shrugged again and leaned into Hunter, who was rubbing his hand up and down her bare back under the blanket.

She would look so good with Hunter's cub in her. Bear agreed, rolling around inside of me, longing to see that happen. Hunter's cub and my cub. And oh my fucking god. I needed to seriously slow the fuck down.

Bear did not agree with that at all, and from the rumble that Hunter was giving off, Beast didn't agree either. My teeth were aching to leave a mark on this girl's skin, and I was mostly positive that the medication she had been on was a suppressant, and she did not know what being an omega even meant.

"My dad's determined," I muttered and looked away. What the fuck were we gonna do? Hunter's eyes were hazy with the pheromones Cassie was putting off. It surprised me I was even still able to think about her wellbeing, with how deep into heat she was falling. "I kinda don't want to talk about it, it will not happen, anyway. Dad just doesn't know it yet." It would not happen, cause Cassie was my omega. No one else would do. I could see that Hunter thought the same way. The gleam in his eyes as he followed the slightly rounded curve of her stomach.

"Oh, okay." She looked down at her hands again, and I felt this kick in my gut. I looked at Hunter, but he was looking at Cassie with lust in his eyes.

I couldn't wait to watch him fuck her. Fuck. She smelled like sugar and slick, and Bear wanted her right now. And I definitely should get up and give her some space before I did something stupid. Things needed clarification before helping any omega through a heat. Especially one who didn't know what was happening to her, as with our sweet Cassie. "So, I really didn't mean to interrupt your time."

"Think nothing of it, princess." Hunter pushed a damp piece of her hair behind her ear and tipped her face up. He gave her all the time in the world to pull away from him. He slowly leaned in to nip at her perfect cupid's bow lips, and she melted into his chest.

Bear crowed.

We had found the girl, our omega. Our beautiful mate.

It wasn't supposed to be possible. Two alphas didn't share a mate, but I could see Beast looking through Hunter's eyes. He watched me as he kissed her, and I could feel that pull from my center, tethering us together. Cassie was ours. And as I pulled away and looked down into her ocean blue eyes, I knew my heart and my soul would be safe.

9

CASSIE

I had absolutely died in the storm, and I was in heaven. Hunter's lips fit perfectly over mine, as he softly sucked at my bottom lip. I sighed into the kiss. I had never had a kiss like that before. My insides were warm and quivery as I could feel it in my belly. I reached up and buried my hands into his thick blond hair and leaned into him, letting the heat of his body set me on fire as he ran his tongue over the seam of my mouth. I opened to him, and when he slipped his tongue inside, I moaned into the kiss running my tongue along his.

I needed more. Dax wasn't there when I reached over to him. I pulled back from Hunter with a smack and looked around. I needed them both to touch me. My skin was on fire, and I knew down to my soul that their touch would make it better.

"Right here, princess," Dax said from behind me. He cupped my cheek in his massive palm and his lips ran over the curve of my neck, pushing me back into Hunter's arms. God, nothing had ever felt that good. "This okay?"

he asked, his lips driving me to distraction as he sucked at the little space behind my ear that apparently lit up everything inside of me and went straight down to my aching middle. All I could do was nod and tip my head to give him more access, but he bypassed my neck and captured Hunter's lips over my shoulder.

Oh, that was so much better. I watched as they battled together over dominance of the kiss, and couldn't help but groan as they trapped me between them. Their bare chests crushing me, each with a hand in my hair, the other on each other. I could live in their embrace forever.

Trapped between them, it was so warm and smelled like Christmas. I never thought Christmas smelled sexy before, but I wanted to do nothing by writhe between them and rub their scents all over my skin. I didn't understand what was happening to my body. Everything felt good and too much, and not enough all at once.

With each biting kiss they shared, the scent only got stronger. I was being bathed in the scent of pine needles and cinnamon and this beautiful citrus bite of oranges and cloves. I couldn't understand where it was coming from, but I never wanted it to stop. Their skin against mine was like silk over stone. Their bodies were so hard. With my breasts pressed tightly against Hunter, and Dax warm at my back, I could do nothing but watch as they kissed, their bodies moving against me in the most amazing ways. My panties were absolutely soaked and feeling incredibly uncomfortable.

They needed to come off.

I needed Hunter and Dax to touch me more. Run their hands down my skin and relieve this ache that had made me feel so hollow inside.

"God, you both are so pretty," I said before I could stop myself, feeling drunk on their presence. Hunter pulled himself away from Dax and chuckled, nipping at my shoulder. Beautiful boys.

"You were right," Hunter said to his boyfriend, with a sly grin on his face. "The perfect omega really exists." He dipped in and nipped at my lips, and I followed him into a deep kiss, chasing Dax's flavor on his tongue.

"What's an omega?" I ask as Hunter broke away.

They both pulled back and just stared at me. Dax tipped my head back - my hair still fisted in his hand - and looked at me with a funny expression.

"Tell me you didn't just say 'what's an omega?'" he growled, a noise that I felt deep inside of me, sending shivers all over my body. He pulled slightly back and turned me to look at him. "Please tell me you're joking."

"No?" I looked back and forth between the two men, but they had both closed down. Something sank inside of me. What had I said? "I mean, I know what omega is, it's a Greek letter, right? And it's like a physics constant? I just finished my exams, and I'm already forgetting everything." I gave a little chuckle, but stopped when they both just kept staring at me like I had suddenly grown a second head, I swallowed hard. Something was very not funny, and it left me on the outside. "Stop looking at me like that." I tried to duck my head away, but Dax's hold on my hair tightened, keeping my eyes directly on Hunter. His face was completely blank. The laughing blue eyes had turned to steel, and I could feel tears prickling, begging to be spilled.

"Where did you say you were from?" Hunter finally asked, his voice low and demanding, pulling something in my belly I didn't understand. All I knew was that I had to answer.

"I grew up on the Veritas Commune." I frowned when Dax suddenly let go of me. Both men got up and started pacing, leaving me alone under the blankets. "Did I do something wrong?"

"No," Dax blurted out, running his hand through his hair and giving Hunter a charged look. "You did nothing wrong. We should have asked, is all."

"I don't understand." I pulled the blanket tightly around myself and felt my stomach drop. It felt wrong and lonely under the blanket by myself. I started shivering again, a whine coming from the back of my throat.

What the fuck was that?

I tried to cover it with a cough, but by the way both of them turned on me, I knew they heard it. I tucked myself further under the blanket, letting the fabric completely consume me. The lingering scent of Christmas helped soothe me, but didn't make me feel any less alone. "Is it cause I'm from Veritas?" Daddy had warned me I could never leave the compound. He said things weren't safe outside. But I felt safe. Hunter and Dax had been nothing like what daddy had said men outside of the compound were like. He'd told me on the outside, men had turned to animals and would hurt me. These men hadn't hurt me at all. They had been kind. But now they were looking at me like I was diseased, and I wanted to vomit. My stomach churned, and a whine pulled from my body.

"Partially." It felt like a kick in my gut and I started whining louder, and couldn't seem to hold it in, or make it stop. Hunter gave Dax another pleading look, but Dax just kept pacing, combing his hands through his hair like something was very, very wrong and he didn't know how to fix it. "Cassie." Hunter sat down next to me and took my hand carefully in his. As his skin met mine, I felt the zap of electricity. I wanted to pull him back under the cover with me and make it better. "I don't know what they taught you at home," he started carefully, lazily rubbing his thumb up and down the back of my hand. "But the world is a lot different from what you know."

"What are you talking about?" I looked back and forth between Dax and Hunter. Dax dropped down next to me on the other side and rubbed his hand up and down my back over the blanket, wrapping me in this feeling of warmth and belonging. They surrounded me with the scent of cloves and pine. The scent caused my insides to turn into only so much goo the closer they got. I fought to pay attention to what they were saying, but this little voice inside of me kept telling me to touch them, make them touch me. We needed their scent. My insides pulsed, and I was so wet, and I ached so much. I didn't want words, I wanted them to make me feel good again. To make this hollowness go away.

"Fuck, darling, there are only a few holdouts that are still living in those compounds," Dax drawled, looking me directly in the eyes. "Most of us have long since started to live in the world again, the compounds didn't keep us from getting the illness that rained down on man after the last war." He shrugged, but kept rubbing my back. "That disease, though; it wasn't lethal, but it did something to our genetics."

"Yeah?" I whispered. "Daddy said it turned men into monsters." I burrowed down under the blanket between them, the heavy scent of Christmas making me feel drunk and loose, and the feel of their hands on me, even though the thick fabric of the blanket warmed me inside. "He said that was why we had to stay on the farm. But then the stranger came." It was so hard to concentrate or resist the urge to rub my face against them.

What was going on?

They needed to be back under the blanket with me, but they stayed on the outside.

"Monsters." Hunter huffed a humorless laugh. "Princess, that's an excellent way to put it." He looked over at Dax and then back down at me. "Whatever chemicals they were using in those bombs they dropped, it messed with our DNA."

"What?" The bombs had dropped illness? Daddy had said the illness was like the plague, sent down to kill everyone. The bombs were from the war. That had happened first, made us weak, then the illness came. "No, it was death."

"Fuck, of course you compound types would learn that." Dax sighed, still rubbing slow circles on my back over the blanket.

I just wanted to crawl all over him. I wonder what he would do if I just grabbed his cock? I mean, it was right there, and all hard and red and angry looking. It wanted me to touch it. I reached out, but Dax stopped me, taking my hand and kissing my palm.

"Cas, you gotta know this." Dax cradled my hand in his, but the grip was firm when I tried to pull away.

"Right." I nodded. Too much. My head just kept bobbing up and down. "What were you saying?"

"Man, Dax." Hunter tucked the blanket around me and scooted back. "She's too far into her pre-heat, dude, she's not gonna be able to say no." His eyes flashed in the lantern light in a way that wasn't at all normal. "We gotta get out of here."

"Too late, Bear's already chosen. Beast has got to be going crazy, too." Dax's voice hit an unfamiliar note, a growl forming in his words.

Maybe daddy was right. These men were like animals, and they were looking at me like I was their next meal. Except I didn't feel scared. I felt excited and really wet. I wanted them to gobble me up.

"You're an omega, Cas, and Hunter and I are your alphas." Dax looked me in the eye, and something shifted in my gut. Made me look down, away from his gaze.

"That doesn't make any sense." I shook my head, but tried again to grab for his long, thick shaft. Something was happening to it. His cock looked like it was getting thicker at the base. That couldn't be normal, right? Maybe he just needed release. I could help him with that. "Can't I just touch you?"

"No." His grip tightened around my wrist, tucking the blanket more securely around me.

I felt like a swaddled infant. I was all alone under the quilt. It felt wrong; I needed to be free; I needed their skin. They should touch me. A whine escaped from my throat. I needed to be touched. I needed not to ache. They were letting me hurt. They were supposed to make me feel better, and they weren't.

"Not until you know what's happening, and you can make an informed decision," he said firmly.

"Dax, there ain't gonna be any informed decision." Hunter rubbed his hands over his hair and hunched in on himself. "I can smell her slick, it's like fucking candy. We either gotta help her, or we gotta leave, and make her ride this out alone."

"Please don't leave me." I hurt so bad, the feeling of emptiness in my belly was overwhelming. "I just want to touch you, I want to feel better."

"That's the omega talking, Cas," Dax said, looking up at Hunter with a helpless expression. "You're our omega and our mate. And as alphas, they built us to take care of you." He ran his cheek along mine, and I felt a little relief. "There was no disease, it was a genetic mutation, turned on some genes and made us different." He licked the side of my neck and I felt another rush of stickiness coating my thighs. It felt so good to be touched. "When we mate you, it'll bind you to us physically for a time, but more. It'll bind us down to our souls, and that's forever."

"Yes, that." I nodded, pulling my hand from his and dropping the blanket from around my shoulders. "Bind us, make this ache stop." I was panting, I needed to touch them.

"Cas, this is forever." Hunter knelt by me, his dick pointing straight at me, the same thickening happening at its base. Why did they look like that? I hadn't seen many naked men, just ones in old art books, but Dax and Hunters were much longer, thicker than any I'd seen. They were shaped differently, and I wanted them in me. "Once we do this, you aren't going back home. You're ours."

"Can't go back home." I finally got my hand around Hunter's dick and squeezed the base. Hunter's head went back and a long growl rumbled from his throat, a bead of white formed at the tip. I leaned down and swiped it with my tongue. The flavor of wood smoke and cloves burst through my mouth along with the musky taste of man. "You're mine, too." I looked up at him between my lashes and sucked the head of his thick cock into my mouth.

10

DAX

I don't think I have ever been so turned on watching someone else get head, but seeing Cassie's pink lips wrapped around Hunter's cock? It was beautiful to witness.

She gripped Hunter's slowly inflating knot in one hand, her other reached back to pull me close. I had not one single objection. I gathered her hair around my fist and draped myself along her spine, my erection pressed firmly between the cheeks of her ass as I whispered in her ear.

"Tighter." I gripped my hand around hers, fisting Hunter's knot in our joined hands, putting more pressure on it. "It's more sensitive to pressure than the rest of his dick." I bit at her ear, feeling her shiver and let Hunter's cock press further into her throat. "That's right princess, relax your throat, let him slide in."

Hunter watched us with hooded eyes, his fists clenching and unclenching with the need to wrap his hands in

Cassie's hair, to be rough with her, the way I knew he liked. I leaned back and slid my cock between her wet folds, testing how ready she was. She was absolutely soaked. I winked up at Hunter and let go of Cassie's hair, letting my hand run down the soft skin of her shoulder and around her ribs to cup her breasts. Hunter's hand wound into her ponytail where I had abandoned it and pulled the long hair tight around his fist.

"Relax princess," Hunter gritted out as he forced her head back farther so he could push just a little deeper down her throat. He pressed forward carefully, with shallow thrusts. I could see her throat working, swallowing around his girth. "I won't hurt you." His words ended in a low growl that riled Bear up something fierce.

I could feel more slick running down between her legs, coating both of us as I teased her with my cock and plucked at her pebbled nipples. "She's so wet." My voice was just as wrecked as Hunter's. She felt fucking amazing. Good mate, Bear growled inside of me. Bite her. The grumble roared up my throat. No, we can't bite her yet. I pushed back at Bear. "Princess, let Hunter go, we need you now."

She let Hunter's cock fall from her perfect lips with a sexy little pop. "Need me?" She panted, tears running down from her baby blues. "Am I not doing this right?"

"You were perfect, princess." Hunter knelt before her, his hands still fisted in her hair, and pulled her lips to his. He sucked at her full bottom lip, leaving little sipping kisses against her mouth. "But if I bust before I'm inside you, it won't help that ache your feeling."

"Get on the bed, man." I plucked at Cassie's nipples one last time, and nipped at her neck, teasing myself. Bear wanted to mark up her pretty neck, tell the entire fucking world that she was ours, but I pushed him back, only scoring my teeth lightly just under her ear. Feeling her shiver against me, tested me further. It would have been so easy to just plunge my cock into her wet heat. "I wanna see her ride you."

"But," Hunter nodded to where I was still thrusting my hips against her. I just shook my head. Hunter should be the first one. I wanted to watch.

God, she smelled fucking amazing. The scent of cinnamon sugar filled my nostrils. Hunter just nodded and took Cassie's hand and led her to our bed. She followed him, but not without looking back at me, and wiggling her fingers for me to take. Good mate. Bear was rolling around inside me, he was so happy. This was perfect.

Hunter helped Cassie up onto the bed, and for the first time since she had stumbled through the door, she looked unsure. "You done this before, princess?" Hunter asked.

Fuck, I should have thought of that. Veritas and those other compounds. They were extremely strict on letting their girls have sex before they were paired. Stupid monster, I growled at myself; the sound vibrating my chest and caused Cassie to gasp.

"You're safe." I crawled up on the bed behind her and rubbed my cheek along the side of her face, leaving calming scent trails on her skin. She relaxed back against me. "Hunter asked you a question."

"No," she whispered. She sounded unsure, but she arched her back, pressing her sex right against my dick, and rubbed her slick all over me. "Daddy." she swallowed hard. "He said that I had to wait until marriage, that dutiful daughters didn't disgrace their daddies." The tip of my cock bumped against her clit, and she moaned. "But I want you to touch me. Please?"

I met Hunter's eyes over her head, and we had a quick discussion. We could make her wait. It would hurt, and she would be miserable trying to ride out her heat with two alphas right there, able to sooth her, but refusing. Or we could claim our mate.

"Dax, back off her man." Hunter held his hand out to me, and I crawled up the bed to him. "Now, Cassie." Hunter grabbed her by the chin gently and looked her directly in the eye. "What is it you want? Cause if you're just trying to make us happy, that ain't gonna to fly."

"I..." she tried to pull her face free of Hunter's grip so she could look away, but he wouldn't let her. "I want you," she whispered so quietly, that if I wasn't a shifter, I would have never heard her.

"I'm sorry, Cas." Hunter rubbed his face against hers, leaving his scent on her. "You wanna say that again like you mean it?"

"I want you," she said louder, her throat jerking convulsively as she swallowed. "I want you both, right now, please." Cassie wrapped her little hands around Hunter's wrists and leaned into him, claiming his lips. "You make me feel good," she breathed against his mouth.

Fuck.

"Okay." Hunter nodded and propped himself up against the headboard. "Come here, then." He helped her straddle his lap. I watched as he ran his hands over her skin, resting them on her hips as he guided her over him, his cock dragging through her wet folds, just like I had been doing moments before. Her tiny little moans were slaying me. "You feel so good princess," Hunter whispered against her hair, as he helped her move over him. "You ready for all of me?" He took himself in hand and rubbed the head of his cock between her thighs, gathering more slick. Her helpless tiny sounds turned deep and needy, her head falling back on her shoulders as she let him move her how he wanted.

"Please Hunter," she sighed, her fingers pulling at his shoulders. "Dax." God, I felt that down in my soul. "Dax come closer, I need you."

"Anything you want, Cas." I straddled Hunter's legs behind her and tucked my cock against her ass, pressing between the round cheeks. I trailed little kisses on her bare shoulders.

Hunter entered her slowly, giving her tiny little thrusts. Her little nails dug into his shoulder as she pulled at his skin, her whines filling the entire room with her need. "She's ready man." I reached around between them and found her little nub. I pressed my thumb to her clit, and she keened. Her back bowed and Hunter pulled her down over him until he was sheathed entirely to the hilt. Cassie's body went tight and rigid. I rubbed at her clit softly until she relaxed and started making the cutest fucking mewling sounds in the back of her throat. "Excellent job, Cas," I mumbled into her ear. Bear was rolling around in elation.

"You good, princess?" Hunter asked, his thumbs rubbing small circles on the outer curve of her hips.

11

CASSIE

The ache dissolved as Hunter pushed deep into me. The thick shaft of his cock dragged along inside of me — touching places I could only even have dreamed of — stretching me with the most beautiful friction. Dax held me in the cradle of his arms, trapping me between my two men, his thumb working against my clit in time with Hunter's thrusts, working to spiral me higher.

"Feels good." It was all I could make myself answer with when Hunter asked me how I was doing. Dax huffed a laugh against my neck and it sent cascading shivers through my entire body.

"Good girl." Dax nipped at my neck and something inside of me unlocked. I wanted his teeth. They needed to be on my neck. Why weren't they in my neck? I needed him to sink his teeth in me, or I would never be complete. I tipped my head to the side and whined, but Dax just shook his head. "You don't know what you're asking, princess." I whined louder, taking my hands from where I had them locked around Hunter's neck, and grabbed Dax by the back of the head. My fingers tugged at his hair, pushing his face into the crook of my neck. I rocked my hips in time with Hunter's thrusts and whined for more.

"Please." The word felt like it was dragging from the depth of my ache. I needed Dax to make it right. I pulled at his hair, not caring if I was ripping it out, I just needed him to put his teeth back on me. Instead, he kissed my skin gently, trailing little soft pecks on my skin. I wanted hard, I wanted pain to even out the pleasure, to keep me from flying off into the ether.

The pressure in my middle was growing with every deep thrust of Hunter's cock, but it wasn't enough. I chased each thrust, pressing myself harder down onto the thickening part of his dick, the part that wasn't quite going inside of me. Each thrust of my hips against it made my insides quake. It would feel so good if it would just go in.

Hunter's hands left my hips and cradled my face. "You're so beautiful, Cassie." He nipped at my lips and pulled me harder onto him, grinding his thick base into my entrance. Once. Twice. And then there was a pop, and it slid in. And my world exploded into rainbow sparkles of pure pleasure.

I let my head drop onto Hunter's shoulder. Finally releasing my death grip on Dax's hair. They smelled so good, like cloves and pine, and just a hint of cinnamon sugar. I turned my face and licked the base of Hunter's throat. My teeth ached. Not in the same way my pussy had, but just as bad. I needed something, and I just couldn't grasp what it was.

I licked at his throat one more time and ground myself down further on him, the thick part of his cock pressing just right inside of me, making that pressure build again.

"Fuck Cas." Hunter kept bucking shallowly inside of me, the fresh burst of his orgasm filling me over and over.

And I bit.

Like a snake. I just pulled my head back and struck. Sunk my teeth into his throat until I tasted iron. "Oh god," he groaned and a fresh wave of cum washed hot against my insides, my body answering his as I ground my teeth into his flesh, his blood running hot down my throat and over my chin.

Dax groaned into my back as he painted my skin with his release. Then there was hot pain on the back of my neck that made my body shudder for a moment. A white hot orgasm pulsed through me, around Hunter's thick shaft. My vision went black for a moment. It felt like dying and finally living all at once.

Warmth trickled down my shoulder from where Dax had bitten me. I released Hunter's skin with a groan. I never wanted to move again. I'd had sex for the first time, and it was glorious. I had bitten a man, had someone bite me hard enough that a river of red was staining Hunter's skin where it touched mine. I should have been concerned, right? But I wasn't. Everything felt right.

"I never want to move," I voiced my thoughts, and both men chuckled.

"You're in luck, Cas." Hunter gathered me further into his arms while Dax licked at the wound on my shoulder. It didn't hurt so much anymore. "We're not going anywhere for a while." Hunter kissed my face, nuzzling his cheek against mine, then Dax did the same.

"Good mate," Dax purred. He lay down beside us, his hand rubbing up and down my spine as he pecked my lips and then Hunter's. "Mine."

12

HUNTER

Cassie jerked awake and tried to pull away from me, but the tie of my knot inside of her pulled painfully. "What on earth?" She looked down between us and pulled again. "Let me go, Hunter." She cried out as she tried a third time. I bit into the inside of my cheek to keep from snarling at her. Fuck, it hurt and sent sparks of pleasure through me making my knot thicken again.

"Cas." I grabbed her hips and fit them snuggly against me, holding her still. "You gotta wait."

"What do you mean?" She struggled in my grip and my fingers bit into her skin hard enough to leave little finger shaped bruises. "I wanna get up." She pushed at my hands. "Hunter, you're hurting me."

"I'm sorry, princess." I took one hand from her hips and shoved Dax, who was drooling in his sleep next to us. "Man wake up."

"Fuck off, dude." He just rolled over and went to go back to sleep, but Cassie was whining, her distress scent turning her cinnamon sugar smell acrid and burnt. Dax had to have smelled it too, cause he was off the bed in a shot, looking around the room for whatever was upsetting Cassie. But it was me. Me and my fucking knot, which she kept pulling at trying to get away. It was seriously not helping, because she was alternating between pulling at our tie and grinding down into me. My knot was fully inflated again. Fuck, I was going to either bleed or come, and it was a toss up which one.

"Princess, you gotta stop." I tried to pull her down and sooth her. If I could work the bite Dax left on her shoulder, she would relax, but she was a wildcat.

"Let me go," she whined, thrashing around in my hold. Fuck. "Hunter, you're hurting me, let me go."

"I know, baby." I caught Dax's eyes over her shoulder, and he finally got it. "Just relax, you're making it worse." I grunted as she ground down against our tie and lit me up. God, it felt good, and the distress hormones coming off our mate was confusing the hell out of my instincts. Beast was freaking the fuck out and turning while I was still tied to her would be a disaster.

Dax climbed up on the bed and sat down behind Cassie. He gathered her hair in one hand and pulled her neck to the side. Not too gently, either. But when his teeth connected with his bite, she went limp in his arms.

"Feels good," she sighed and stopped struggling. "Dax, that feels so good."

Dax ran his tongue over the mostly healed bite and locked eyes with me. "Yeah, darling." Dax laid a kiss on the mark and ran his hand over her arms until she settled against my chest again. "We're your alphas, remember what we talked about?"

"Kinda," she whispered against my neck. Her tongue reached out and ran over the bite on my shoulder, and I shuddered. "No, not really."

"Okay, we need to talk about what happened then." Dax sighed. "To start, I want you to know that you're completely safe with us." Dax pulled the blanket up, tucked it over us.

"Not a brilliant way to start." Her voice was half drunk, but she still went to push away from me. I pulled her back to me and ran my tongue over the raised bite. It was Dax's mark, so I shouldn't have been able to sooth her, but she relaxed right back into me. The walls of her pussy fluttered around my knot, and I ground my teeth, resisting the urge to pump into her. Tease her back into that heat smell. "That is not the way to put someone at ease, so excuse me while I reserve an opinion."

"Sorry." Dax huffed and looked at me again. "We should have explained this better."

"What he means to say is we're sorry we didn't explain better beforehand." He gave me an exasperated look, and I shrugged back at him. "We are terrible at this, aren't we?"

"Yes." Cassie rolled her eyes at the both of us, but rubbed her cheek against mine, instincts making her mark me with her scent. I must smell upset, too. "Okay, how about we start simple?"

"Right." Dax nodded. "We're alphas, which means when we have sex with an omega, and we are ready to climax, there is this part of our penis..."

"Dude, you make it sound so clinical," I shoved him, knocking Dax over with ease, he just flopped to the bed next to us, making the bed rock. Man, my knot was never going down at this rate. And I could already smell Cassie's heat hormones building up again. "The thing at the base of our cocks is called a knot, it locks into an omega and keeps our seed in you longer, so we can breed." I turned to Dax. "See, not so hard."

"I don't know about you, but I'm hard as fuck," Dax growled. I ignored him.

"Like a wolf?" Cassie looked weirded out, even though we were literally tied together, and she was subtle rocking her hips against our tie. I could feel her slick leaking out around my knot, and it was making it really hard to think. And I really needed to.

"The DNA that got unlocked?" Dax looked at Cassie with meaning. Right, that thing we were talking about before she decided that sucking my cock down her throat was way more important than listening. I rubbed the bite mark on my shoulder. I probably should have made her listen. "It unlocked animal stuff. The dynamics, alpha, beta and omega. There are gammas too, but very few, and they're different."

"You suck at this," I sassed, which was met with rolling eyes from both Dax and Cassie.

"Alphas are what Hunter and I are, we're bigger, more aggressive, and have knots, which is why you and Hunter are stuck right now. And we're built specifically to mate with omegas, which is what you are."

"Good job asshole, she was relaxing." Plus her heat scent that had been filling the cabin, receded again, and she had tugged at our tie again. Man, it hurt when she tried to pull away.

"And it absolutely terrified me," Cassie whined. Her heat and distress warring in the air.

Man, this was messing with Beast. I couldn't let him out until my fucking knot went down, and if she kept moving around and pulling at us, it wasn't going to. A low growl rattled up my throat, and I tried to swallow it down. Cassie looked down at me with wide eyes.

"Sorry, princess." I bit the inside of my cheek so hard I tasted copper.

"And if you had let us talk and stopped giving off those fucking delicious pheromones, and hadn't grabbed Hunter's dick, we would have explained." Dax grumbled and then inhaled a lengthy breath and continued, Bear's silver grey eyes shining in our mate's face. "Then there are betas, they're like the peacemakers, no knots, not so big and muscley. Gammas are like drones, they take traits of those around them. Finally, there are omegas." Dax leaned in and brushed his cheek against Cassie's. I was almost surprised that she let him, but she leaned into the touch like she was starving for it. "You are one of those. Built to take an alpha's knot, and breed with us. You're in heat. I know you ain't feelin' it right now, but since my bet is that you've been on suppressants, it'll be intense, and it'll rear up again, soon. What you've been feeling, that needy ache, that's heat. When an alpha meets an omega that smells right, we can mate them. A bite forms a bond. If the bond takes, we can breed."

"You bit me." Cassie ran her fingers over the healing bite again. I could already see it scarring around the edges.

"And you bit me," I countered, lounging on the bed. Cassie wasn't struggling anymore. Just sitting on my hips looked concerned. "Your alpha's teeth against the mark will help calm you, and our saliva is made to help sooth you, and help you heal. That's why the bite is almost completely healed, even if it's only hours old."

"Right."

I rubbed my fingers over where Cassie had marked me. The bite on my neck felt healed, just a scar, I could feel the little edges. It made Beast so happy, pushing at my skin to touch her. He was practically drunk inside me.

"If a bite heals and doesn't leave a scar, the bond isn't true." Dax pointed to my neck. "We set our bond. Yours is scarring, too."

"And that means?" Her voice was growing quiet again, and I wanted her to be our fiery mate again, the one who pulled chunks of Dax's hair out trying to force him to do what she wanted. I wanted her teeth on me, and to feel her little claws raking down my skin. Beast didn't like her making herself smaller. And he didn't like the scent of her unease.

"Complications?" I hedged, rubbing my neck, a rumbling coming from my chest. "Two alphas aren't supposed to bond one omega. It's usually one omega, one alpha, and then a couple of betas." I leaned over and rubbed my face against Dax's, sharing our scent, "We thought we would lose each other, when Dax bonded an omega. Alphas get real territorial about their mates, only sharing them with their betas. Never with another alpha."

We had shared just fine, though. "So we're mated? I'm supposed to marry some guy on Monday. You realize that this all sounds insane, right?" Cassie threw her hands up into the air. "I mean, we met, what? Yesterday? Because I got lost in a storm. This is crazy."

"Yeah, saying it out loud, it sounds crazy." Dax deflated and sagged to the bed, curling too, his chin rubbing at the top of my head. I could feel Bear's satisfaction, but also his confusion. "But that doesn't change what happened last night."

"Just." Cassie ran her hand over her head, rubbing the healed mark on her neck. My heart fluttered wildly in my chest, watching her caress Dax's claim.

"Tell me you felt nothing." I slid my hands up her body and down her arms. I looked up at her. She sat so still, looking down at me curiously. "Tell us you didn't feel a connection with us, and we'll drop this and get you back to Veritas." It would kill me to leave my mate, our mate. But I would, if that's what she wanted.

"How?" Cassie mumbled down at her lap. "The road isn't any less muddy than it was last night, it's still pouring. And Veritas won't take me back, anyway. I left, and now I'm tainted." She looked back at me and sucked in a breath, apparently hearing what she had said. "I didn't mean it like that." She tucked a strand of hair behind her ear and looked away. "I mean, to them, being on the outside means I'm diseased. They won't let me back, and even if they did, they would shun me."

"We get it, princess." I took her hand and placed a small kiss to her palm. "Veritas thinks that women are only meant for their husbands. But, mate is a stronger bond than marriage. We want you. We can feel the pull now, everything in you connects to us. Can you feel it?"

"Yeah, I feel something," she said after a lengthy pause, not looking up at either of us. "I'm not saying that I understand this omega thing, but I feel a connection. I'm not running and screaming, right?"

"We'll ease you into it." Dax rubbed his face in his hands. "I mean, really slowly, but Monday we gotta go back home."

"Home? I'm going with you?" she asked. Her face all scrunched up in confusion. We really weren't explaining any of this right.

"When we bond to our mate, we do it for life." I look over at Dax, giving him a tight smile. Beast had finally stopped pressing at my skin, and my shoulders relaxed. "Your tiny little human teeth shouldn't have been able to scar me, but here it is." Dax reached out to her, and she leaned into his touch.

"Human?" Cassie rubbed her cheek against Dax's hand, like she had mine. Possessive mate. Her face went a little slack; he dug his nails into her scalp.

"Fuck." Dax leaned in and nuzzled along her neck. "You guys still tied?" He asked me, Bear looking out at me.

"Nope." I sat up and kissed Cassie's lips and then helped her off my lap. Her hip popped as she stretched. Which was an excellent reminder of why we usually knotted from behind. She scrunched her little nose up and stretched her back. Man, she was cute.

"We got one more thing to show you, darling." Dax slipped off the bed and disappeared into the tiny bathroom. He came back with a damp cloth, and parted Cassie's thighs, carefully washing her. I could smell just a hint of blood mixed in with my release and hers. I soothed Beast, reminding him that she wouldn't bleed next time. "You wanna show her, or me?"

"You can." I picked up my discarded t-shirt from the floor and pulled it over her head. Beast had settled enough that I wasn't worried about turning. I picked up my boxers and tugged them on. When she stood up my shirt nearly fell down to her knees. Man was she cute. I pulled her to the door of the cabin, letting her and Dax out before I pulled the door closed.

"What are we doing out here?" She let me gather her into my arms, relaxing into my body as I nipped at Dax's bite. I would leave one right next to it. I nuzzled my nose against it, and Beast rumbled contentedly.

"Just remember," I whispered against her neck. "Remember, that no matter what, we still love you."

"You love me?" Her voice was so quiet the rain almost drowned out the words. I grazed my teeth over her bite, and she shivered.

"Of course we do, darling." Dax stepped into the driving rain, shaking his head like a dog as his hair soaked and plastered around his shoulders. "You're our mate, our omega."

"You fit with us, princess," I whispered against the side of her neck, tightening my arms around her waist. "And we fit with you. I get to keep both of you. I'm a fucking lucky bastard." Beast agreed.

Cassie just nodded, snuggling further into my arms, her eyes locked on where Dax was standing naked in the rain. "Okay, so what are you showing me that we have to be in the rain?"

"You ready, man?" Dax lifted his brows at me. I nodded, my teeth running over Cassie's claim, keeping her calm. Her cinnamon scent turned sugary and sticky sweet. Her heat was rearing up again. Candy sweet slick perfuming the air. "That animal DNA? It unlocked more for some of us than others."

"What?" Cassie looked from Dax to me, then back at Dax as he let Bear out.

Dax's skin shredded as fur rolled over him. Within moments a dark brown Kodiak bear stood before us. Cassie went completely ridged in my arms, her breath locked in her throat. I bit down on her mark, grinding my teeth just this side of breaking the skin, until she relaxed again and her smell went sweet again.

"Daddy said that the men outside were monsters." Her words came out on a hushed breath, but her hands petted up and down my arms like she was comforting me.

"Cas, that's still Dax," I whispered, nuzzling her neck. My tongue bathing her mark gently. "He just looks a little different now. But inside, it's Dax."

"He's a bear," she breathed. Dax took one lumbering step towards us, and Cassie's little fingers dug into my arms until her nails almost broke the skin. "He's so big."

"We call his bear, Bear." I kissed her cheek.

"Unoriginal." I could almost hear her eye roll. "Are you a bear, too?"

"Yeah, princess, I'm a bear, too."

"What are you called, Bear Two?" Her nails slowly released my skin, and she turned to look at me.

"My bear is Beast, cause of his size." I just shrugged up one shoulder. There was a reason I was Sergeant at Arms. Beast was a beast. "You wanna meet Bear?" I asked, leaving a last kiss on her claiming mark, and feeling her shiver against me.

"He's not going to hurt me, is he?" she whispered. I knew Dax could hear us, but she didn't. There was so much she didn't know.

"Never." I took one of her hands and led her into the rain. Bear was soaked through, sitting there with his ass in the muddy lawn, just waiting. "You're his mate. He would never hurt you. Remember, it's just Dax."

"Right." She nodded too quickly, her heart rate tripping. "Just Dax. Dax is a bear." She took a long breath. "My mates are bear men."

"Bear shifters," I corrected with a small chuckle.

She stopped a few feet away from Bear and pressed back into my chest. "Dax?" Bear canted his head. "I'm going to pet you now." He nodded and lowered his head until it was below hers. It took her three tries to touch him, but finally her fingers ghosted over the coarse wet fur of our mate, and I relaxed. It was all going to be okay.

13

DAX

Hunter and Cassie lay sleeping peacefully, curled up together on the bed. The sunlight streamed across their bodies, just barely covered by the bedsheets. My claim on Cassie's neck had turned to a pink scar that nearly blended into her perfect porcelain skin. Hunter's was white. It sat just over the rolling tendrils of tattoo ink on his shoulder. And I felt a ping of jealousy that he had her claim on him, and my neck was still bare.

I watched them sleep before turning back to the stove. I rarely cooked. And with good reason. I sucked at it. Alphas were not built to be domestic. We were built to defend our pack, keep our mates and cubs safe. But cooking was not in my skill set.

I had this pit in my stomach while I stood at the ancient wood stove and attempted breakfast. When it was just me and Hunter, I didn't bother making proper food. We were both content with a cold protein shake or a bar, nothing special. Our animals needed more protein than a normal human, so we always had stashes of protein bars shoved in odd places, just in case we needed them. Cassie had taken one look at my lemon poppyseed protein bar and turned up her nose. She was so fucking cute.

I figured offering her a chocolate shake for breakfast probably wouldn't go over that well.

So, I was trying my damndest to scramble powdered eggs. I hadn't even known that we had powdered eggs until I had gone rifling through the cabinets above the sink. The powder hadn't looked overly appetizing. Once I added water and heated it over the stove? Yeah, it looked like donkey vomit.

I checked the expiration date on the box of powder for the tenth time, but nope, it was still good. Apparently that was how they were supposed to look. That didn't seem right. I stirred it a few more times with the fork I had found stuffed in the back of the junk drawer, before I gave up.

I scraped the pile of crap into the trash can and hooked my hands on my hip. Shit. "We didn't really shop for company," I said to Hunter as he curled his arms around my waist and set his chin on my shoulder.

"Nope," he agreed. The rumbling growl of Beast's contentment vibrated up my back and Bear answered. It felt different now. Bear felt less wild, less out of control. He had always been calmer around Hunter, but now he was positively zen. "We have the rabbits you brought in last night?" he offered.

"Then what will we eat for dinner?" I asked, all I got was a shrug. Bear had been an excellent mate. After Cassie and Hunter had gone back in the cabin, I had gone hunting. We couldn't just change right back. It put too much strain on the body. And with the newly formed mating bonds, Bear needed to hunt. He needed to make sure we provided for our mate. But cereal wasn't something that was easily hunted for. Which had led me to the egg vomit.

"I don't need anything fancy," a sleepy voice came from the other side of the room and we were treated to Cassie sitting up in bed, stretching her arms over her head, pushing those perfect tits together. I looked over at Hunter, and I could see he was thinking the same thing as I was. Breakfast could wait. We had a mate to satisfy. Her heat scent was strong, and just as alluring as those sexy ass curves of hers.

14

CASSIE

The scent of sulfur or possibly rotting eggs burning woke me from sleep.

I rolled over and watched the two most perfectly muscled backs sway together at the wood stove, Hunter waved away the smoke from the pan I'm pretty sure Dax had just ruined. I took a moment and traced the lines of ink on their backs. Who knew that something like that would entice me, but everything about them did. They both had the same tattoo covering most of their backs. A fearsome looking skull with wings, with a banner above and below. One reading 'Kodiak Bear MC' and the other 'Bear Peak Original.' It looked just like the patches on the back of their vests. Which I had been told were called cuts.

The boys had let me trace each one of their tattoos the night before, once Dax had come back. Telling me about each one. Including the bear outlines that they both wore over their hearts. For each other. My heart had melted when they told me that.

Hunter had successfully distracted Dax away from making anymore of the vile concoction he had been burning on the stove. And the two were whispering. Quietly enough that I couldn't hear what they were saying.

I thought about crawling back under the covers, but my stomach rumbled, reminding me I hadn't eaten in quite some time.

"I don't need anything fancy." I sat up and stretched my back, when I caught a bit of their conversation about food.

They both turned and got this wild look on their faces, their eyes going to the fascinating silver color that told me their bears were close to the surface. Together they stalked across the small cabin toward the bed. I froze as I watched their muscles ripple and move with an animal grace. My goodness, they were beautiful. The scent of pine and clove drowned out the stinky egg smell and made my head spin.

Slick ran between my legs. I needed them both right now. That hollow feeling settled between my thighs, and I knew that my body was readying for a knot. It was such a bizarre thought, but I wanted them to fill me until I couldn't handle any more. I wanted them both inside of me, filling all the little empty spaces. My thighs were sticky with my slick by the time they were halfway across the room, and any thought of food had left my mind.

"I think breakfast is served, what do you think, Dax?" Hunter reached the bed first and ripped the cover away. I was a little embarrassed by the little squeak that escaped from my throat. Dax grabbed my ankle and pulled me to the edge of the bed, a feral grin on his lips. He winked at me, licking his lips. "What do you think, princess?"

"Um." I looked between Dax and Hunter, but never had time to answer. Dax pulled my legs over his shoulders, biting the inside of each of my thighs before leaving a soft kiss right over my clit. Slick soaked into the sheets under me. Dax ran his tongue through my wet folds, and I was done for. I grabbed handfuls of his thick brown hair and rolled my hips against his face. He delved his tongue between my lips and ate at my core. Nothing had ever felt that good. I was sure of it.

Hunter crawled onto the bed above me, and I pulled one hand free of Dax's hair to reach for him. "You just let our mate take care of you, princess." He curled up beside me, his head resting on his hand. "You let us take care of you." His fingers pinched at my nipples hard while he left sweet sucking kisses on my face and shoulders.

"Please." I curled my fingers down Hunter's chest and took his thickening erection into my hand, pulling firmly like Dax had shown me. "I feel so empty." I mewled.

"Looks like your heat is coming back, princess." Hunter cupped my hand in his and fucked himself into the circle of our fists. "What can I do for you?" He leaned in and licked and kissed down my neck.

"That." I arched my neck so he could reach where Dax's mark was. "I want you here. Please." Dax's fingers took over for his lips and he looked up my body to me. Our eyes caught.

"Don't you make the prettiest picture?" Dax kissed the skin just below my belly button. "So fucking sexy." He stood over us, his cock long and thick, fully erect, the base thickening even more. "You gonna make me match our mate? Huh, darling." He kissed the bite mark on my neck and leaned in, rubbed the head of his dick between my folds. All I could do was nod as more slick flowed out of me, soaking the head of his cock. "Hunter?"

"Yeah?" Hunter lifted his head from my neck and pulled me into his arms, so my legs fell to either side of his. "She all ready for you?"

"Bite her good," Dax pressed me back into Hunter's chest, so we were both lying on the pillows at the top of the bed, the thick roll of Hunter's cock pressed tight between the cheeks of my rear end. He thrust shallowly, wetting my back with his pre-cum. Dax kissed Hunter hard and pressed the head of his cock into my soaking pussy.

"More." I turned my head to lick the seam of their lips, where they were joined. "More, please."

"You heard our mate." Hunter pulled away first and went back to bathing my neck with wet kisses, his fingers walking down to where Dax and I were joined. He pressed two fingers hard against my distended clit and rubbed in time with Dax's shallow thrusts. "Harder, she will not go off until you're hitting her with your knot."

"Patience," Dax purred as he gave me an inch more. I arched my back, trying to get more in me, but he pressed his hand into my belly, holding me still. He bent forward and sucked one of my nipples into his mouth, then let it go with a pop. "It'll feel better if you let it build, baby girl." He took the nipple back between his lips and scraped at it with his teeth.

"Please, please," I chanted, writhing between my men. The thickness of Hunter's cock riding between the globes of my backside, and I could feel him stiffening, matching the pace I was trying for, fucking along my back and leaving wetness in his wake. "More, Dax." I panted and twisted, trying to get what I needed, but Dax kept his thrusts shallow enough that I couldn't even feel his knot.

Hunter pinched at my clit as he fucked against my back, his teeth scoring my neck and shoulder. "Man, come on," he growled at Dax, grabbing at the other man's hair with his free hand. "Fuck her, damn it." His teeth played me like a fine-tuned instrument, keying me up to the point I almost missed it when Dax reared back and then shoved his cock all the way in, his knot slipping right into the tight opening of my pussy. Fire erupted through me with such force I was sure I blacked out, because the next thing I knew, Dax's neck was giving way under my teeth, and all I tasted was his blood and pure satisfaction.

"Cassie," Dax sighed, his weight falling onto me, pressing both of us back into Hunter, who was licking the blood flowing from the fresh bite on my throat. "Mate."

15

DAX

Hunter snored quietly, his face tucked up against Cassie's chest. She ran her fingers through his thick dirty blond hair, and he sighed, rubbing his stubble against her like a great big cat. It was beautiful watching them together. Bear agreed. The feeling of our tether, the bond connecting us made my animal calm and excited at the same time. I hadn't been ready for marriage, but I loved the bond with Cassie more than anything. Fuck, she gave me everything that I never thought I would get to have.

"How did you know?" Cassie tipped her head back against my chest. I had been carefully braiding and unbraiding her hair for the better part of an hour, while Hunter slept. My fingers scraped against her scalp, drawing soft moans that made my heart full. I'd been telling her about claiming gifts, and how I wished I had something to give her. She insisted she didn't need gifts, but I wanted to spoil her. Bear wanted to spoil her with everything.

"How did I know, what?" I hummed, pulling a tiny braid out of her hair and running my fingers through the freed strands. I would buy her combs for her hair. Beautiful silver ones, like the ones my dad had gotten my mother when they were courting. They wouldn't be practical for days that we took the bike, but they would please my mate.

She had grown up on a commune, completely sheltered from the real world. There were so many things Hunter and I could introduce her to, that she would never have had. Most communes didn't have the simple things, like fuel for cars, or access to parts. The fact that she had even had a car to steal to escape was fucking amazing. Let alone that she had driven it. Women were second-class citizens, only carrying their husband's status. Cassie's father must be pretty important to have a car. So, what had made him sell his only daughter?

"How did you know I was what you were looking for?" She curled her fingers into Hunter's hair, and I never wanted to move again. Watching her touch him was heaven, her letting me touch her was just icing on an already perfect cake. "How did you know I'd work with both of you, and this wasn't just desperation grabbing at something?"

"Well, your teeth marked up Hunter and my necks, so there's that." I shrugged and selected a few pieces of hair and started braiding again. "My dad told me it felt like an electric shock, like static electricity, when you touched your true mate. A good match will smell right, but a genuine match, a destined mate? That person you feel down to your bones. And when you touched me, you lit me up inside."

Static. Fuck, that's what it had felt like when Hunter touched me that first time, but that had been so long ago and we had been so young, that I had never really thought about it. We had been best friends since we were very young. His dad had been Sergeant at Arms, and now Hunter was. And one day, when dad was gone or too old, I would be the Prez.

Hunter still made little sparks dance along my skin when we touched, and when I had touched Cassie, the first time everything had clicked. That quick spark that made Bear lay down and watch from inside me, and finally I felt like I could be whole.

"But your dad was fixing you up with a mate?" she asked. Curious mate.

"I think he's worried." I pulled her close, my arm around her shoulders, my chin resting on the crown of her head. Slowly, I breathe in her scent. Now that we were mated her scent had changed. She told me we smelled like Christmas. To me, we just smelled like home, the piny woods, and the cabin, and cinnamon rolls in the morning. I rocked her as I thought, watching her fingers trace the lines of ink that adorned my arms. "It's getting too close, and I haven't been looking."

"'Cause of Hunter?" Cassie's fingers walked through Hunter's hair again, and something settled inside of me. Her heat scent was still present, but not as intense as it had been. She smelled sated, and Bear was proud. "And now?"

"Now." I sighed and kissed the top of her head, sliding down a little on the bed and pulling her against my chest. "Bonding differs from just mating. Bonding means the bear chooses too. It's forever." I traced the claiming marks on her neck. Two sets of thin scars from Hunter and my teeth, set together like interlocking circles. She shivered as I touched them, and her scent warmed, rousing the heat scent again. Her heat wasn't over. We had a few more days of the rolling tides of heat urging us to mate.

"So we're bonded," Cassie said, looking up at me, her eyes growing hazy and heavy as I lazily drew the circles of her claim.

"Fuck darling, we are so bonded." I sighed, enjoying the weight of her body against mine. "The three of us? We're mated and bonded. We are a unit, and you are our everything." I kissed the crown of her head, she smelled so good covered in our scents.

This was complicated, this was unknown territory for all three of us. I held her gently for a long moment, and we both looked down at Hunter, carefully touching him while he slept. It was the most right I'd ever felt, just curled up with Cassie, Hunter sleeping beside us.

"You're really bonded to a couple of biker bears," I said after a lengthy pause, seeing the happiness in her eyes. Both Cassie and Hunter were mine, and it felt like everything. I didn't want some girl my dad had promised to me, and couldn't bond her now, anyway. Maybe it was the devil you know, but it felt good to be with them and feel the security that came with the bond.

"And you're mated to a little sheltered princess," she countered, her eyebrow raised in a tease.

"Yep, and you're our princess now. Princess of the Kodiak Bear Pack. And one day, you're gonna be queen." Her heat scent was overwhelming me again, the room was filling with it. And while I knew I should feed her, Bear wasn't ready to let our mates out of bed yet. "We should wake Hunter."

"Will you make me stop hurting?" she asked quietly, her fingers now pulling at Hunter's hair, her hips working against his back, looking for relief.

"You read my mind, princess." I cupped her face in my hand and pulled her to me. Her lips were soft and gentle against mine. The kiss was slow, like we had the rest of our lives.

CASSIE

Dax stuffed what was actually salvageable from my duffle into his saddlebags. "That's everything, darling." He leaned across the bike and gave me a peck on the cheek. "You sure you're feeling up to riding?" That wasn't the first time Dax had asked. I was a little sore. My heat ended up lasting for six full days, and once the heat hormones subsided, by body ached everywhere. Not the way it had during the heat. But sore like overworked muscles. Muscles I never even knew I had.

"I'm fine, Bear." I touched the concentric scars on my neck and smiled. Sore or not, I was happy. "Take me home."

"Anything for you." Dax looked so different in his ripped jeans and leather cut. They had explained that it was called a cut, but to me it looked like a vest, with all kinds of patches and things attached to it. Hunter had been very patient, explaining each unique thing on the cut and what it meant, along with a bunch of other information about my new life. Most of it had drifted away in the heat. Some of it had stuck, though. "We'll have to get you a helmet when we get back." He fitted his own helmet on my head, his tongue sticking out the side of his mouth as he adjusted the straps to fit more snuggly. "I don't like how loose this is on you, baby girl." He rattled the helmet around, before fisting his hands onto his hips and thinking. "We'll just have to take it slow."

"Looking good Cas." Hunter jumped down the porch steps and sauntered over to us. He wrapped me up in his arms as soon as he was close enough. "Red is definitely your color." He smacked me on my ass. "Glad this all fits you right."

My clothes had been mostly a lost cause. I had dropped my bag while trying to get to the cabin the first night, and by the time Beast found them on one of his excursions, they had been mostly ruined. Dax had unearthed a few items from his saddlebags, a pair of bright red, skin-tight jeans, and a tank top that was bordering on indecent, and my vest, which I was assured was called a vest, and it buttoned under my breasts, pushing them up and together. It all belonged to one of the girls back at the club. Though, my boobs were practically spilling out of the top, making me a little worried that they would pop free at any moment. The boys didn't seem to have the same concern.

"They're fine." I shrugged. They smelled like Dax, and that had helped. That they belonged to another woman, which bothered me, but I was his mate, and she was just another woman who lived in the same compound he did. That had not made me feel comfortable in the tight fitting clothing.

"We'll send you shopping after we get settled." Dax reassured me.

I still didn't fully understand the way the dynamics of my new life worked. I was still trying to wrap my head around the fact that while Dax, Hunter and I were mated, there would still be these other people in our lives and part of our pack. My entire world had changed overnight. From scared children in a compound meant to keep us from discovering what was in the outside world, to one of comfort and ease in this brave new world that had formed since humanity had been changed. The world had evolved and it didn't matter how much momma and daddy stuck their heads in the sand and tried to ignore it, we had changed as well.

"Right." I pulled away from Hunter and tugged at the strap of my helmet, trying to get it to fit more snuggly. "Let's just get going?"

"Darling." Dax gently took my hands away from the helmet straps and held them gently in both of his. "I know this is all a lot for you, but I promise, everything is going to be alright. It's just going to take some getting used to."

"As long as you're there, it'll be fine. Just nerves." I desperately was trying to convince myself. In the cabin, hidden away from the world it was safe, but the idea of being around new people? The teachings of my father hadn't disappeared overnight. So many humans meant disease, right? "It's just not how I was raised."

"I know." He gently tugged on my arms until I relented, and let him pull me into his embrace, tucking me up against his chest, wrapping me up in his scent. "But just meet them first?" I just wound my arms around his waist and nodded. "This is all going to be a learning curve, Cas, for all of us."

"Okay." I looked up at him, his eyes the warm silver that told me Bear was close to the surface. "I can do this."

"The club will be so excited to meet our mate, you'll be the talk of the town for sure." Hunter hugged me up from the other side, sandwiching me between my two alphas. "And it'll be good for the girls to have another female around. The MC is a boys' club. They'll finally have someone to hang out with when we're gone, that isn't a Kitten, the MC girls do not get along with most of the Kittens. They are a bunch of catty bitches, according to them."

Ugh, the concept of the Kittens was even more strange than the idea of living free in the world. Kittens were the girls that hung around the clubhouse and were basically fair game for any member looking to get their dick wet - Dax's words - they weren't attached to any one member. The thought of one of them hanging off Dax or Hunter just made my stomach sick to my stomach. "I'm sure they're right." It made me like the idea of meeting these girls more, if they weren't a fan of the Kitten concept either. Gag.

"Hey." Hunter tipped my head up to look at him. "We don't touch the Kittens." He had said that before, but I wasn't sure how much I believed him. "Cassie, Dax and I don't fuck the Kittens. We have each other and now we have you. And you are most important of all. You are our mate, you come first. The Kittens are for the members that don't have their own mates. We have you and each other. We do not need to look at the Kittens for anything except getting our drink orders, and half the time they fuck even that up." He looked down at me, his eyes serious. "You are our mate, Cassie. You come first in everything. Okay?"

"Okay." He bent down and kissed me. He tasted like pine and wood smoke, and I couldn't help but open my lips to him. Any time my alphas touched me, I felt so loved and cherished. His tongue swept into my mouth, rubbing down alongside my own, and I was awash with comfort and calm. "Okay," I said again when he pulled back, but that time I felt more like I meant it.

"Good." Hunter nodded and cupped my ass, holding me tight to him, so I could feel the hard length of his erection against my stomach. "Have I told you how hot you look?"

"Once or twice." I leaned my head against his chest and held him to me, Dax's too large helmet only partially ruining it. "But you can say it again."

"You look hot, darling." Dax called from where he was checking the cabin one last time before we left. "You'll look even better when you wear our cut. Our sexy omega, rocking the Kodiak Bear MC colors." He gave me a sexy boy wink. I was getting my cut, and on the back it would say 'Property of Dax and Hunter' and that was something that I wanted. I wanted everyone to know who my alphas were. The world at large I was iffy on, and the trampy Kittens in the clubhouse, I could have lived without. But wearing my mate's brand along with their marks? That I wanted.

"Take me home, Bear?" I reluctantly pulled away from Hunter and took Dax's outstretched hand.

"Let's go home."

THE END

ACKNOWLEDGMENTS

My lovely readers,

This novella was a labor of love during the start of the pandemic. It gave me a space to write something that would take me out of the world for a little while. I'm so excited to give you all an updated version of Secret Omega, ready for the wide world to read. Lots of things have changed since I originally wrote this in 2020, but what hasn't is my love for the story itself.

None of this would be possible without the incredible support from my friends and fellow authors, who have done nothing but encourage me, help me grow as a writer, and push me to try things outside of my comfort zone.

First, I want to thank Miri Stone. Our friendship grew like a beautiful garden through those first extremely hard months of the pandemic. We held each other's hands through some of the worst of it, and I can't thank her enough for that friendship.

Through Miri I met Mariah Thayer, who has become a soul sister. Her support, encouragement, and unwavering love has been such a boon in some of my hardest moments.

I started chatting with Shelly Ferguson after she joined on to my first (and only) Christmas Anthology. Her warm heart and often devious mind cemented our bond, and I can't imagine being without her and her sassy, sarcastic ass.

Last, but certainly not least, I have to thank T.K. Eldridge, who has been gently but firmly shoving me out of the Zon box. Her handholding has helped me realize that the Great and Powerful Oz isn't the be all and end all of the indie publishing world. I can't thank her enough for her kind nudging and plentiful knowledge in all that is indie. She has been and continues to be a valuable friend and wise mentor.

Of course, I can't forget my readers. You all are why I do what I do. Why I pour my heart and soul into each one of these books, and push myself beyond the boundaries of what I thought possible. I love you all.

XOXO,

Kat

P.S.—If you're curious about more of my books, or are looking to get updated on the crazy things I get up to (spoiler - its really just my characters who find all the drama) you can jump over to my website or my newsletter for more up to date goings on in all my worlds!

ABOUT THE AUTHOR

If you're looking for steamy paranormal romance, you've come to the right place. K.O. Newman writes everything from gods and monsters to fairies and shifters.

When she's not immersed in her own fantasy world, K.O. is a mom to two little boys, and wife to a fantastic man. She lives outside of St. Louis in southern Illinois, and spends her days working with seniors at a retirement community.

Writing is in her bones. K.O. has been toiling with stories since she was old enough to hold a book, despite struggling with dyslexia. She started writing fanfiction in highschool, and quickly began to grow her own characters and stories. Her mind is constantly filled with new friends (and steamy book boyfriends) that she can't wait to share.

Check out my Website for more.

ALSO BY K.O. NEWMAN

Lords Of Khaos Series

Malachai

Lesleigh

Cherry

Finnegan

Fitzgerald (coming soon)

Standalones

Secret Omega

Reclaiming Psyche

Autumn Curses

Wish

With Mariah Thayer

Blood Moon Riders Series

Crow Moon

Pink Moon

Flower Moon

Hot Moon

Thunder Moon

Omnibus One

Witches of Winter Haven

Wing Witch (Coming Soon)

With Miri Stone

Soul of the Chaos

Bartender Mate (Coming Soon)

With Shelly Ferguson

Ember (Coming Soon)